PATRICIA FORDE
BUMPFIZZLE THE BEST ON PLANET EARTH

ILLUSTRATED BY ELĪNA BRASLIŅA

BUMPFIZZLE THE BEST ON PLANET EARTH

First published in 2018 by
Little Island Books
7 Kenilworth Park
Dublin 6W
Ireland

First Published in the USA in 2022

ISBN: 978-1-915071-21-7

A British Library Cataloguing in Publication record for this book is available from
the British Library

Designed and typeset by Catherine Gaffney

Printed in Poland by Drukarnia Skleniarz

Little Island receives financial assistance from the Arts Council of Ireland /An
Chomhairle Ealaíon

10 9 8 7 6 5 4 3 2 1

For my mother, Detta Forde,
who taught me to read.

This is the very, very, *very* important diary of the very, very, *very* important warrior: Bumpfizzle the Best

NOTE

If you are <u>not</u> a Plonker – KEEP OUT!

If you <u>are</u> a Plonker – KEEP OUT!

If you are WHIZZPIFFLE or ANY of her gang – KEEP RIGHT OUT!

OCTOBER 15TH

I have written my first official report to the Great Master.

To: Great Master, Planet Plonk
From: Warrior Bumpfizzle the Best
Subject: Field Report

Oh Great Master Hornswoggle!

I arrived safely on Earth on Monday. Our quest for new friends has begun! I have taken the form of an earthling boy, aged ten years, and have performed a memory-adjustment on the host family. They now believe that they gave birth to this child ten Earth winters ago, whereas in fact, as you know, this boy was hatched in Lab 6675 four hundred light years ago. They also believe that my name is Daniel. Hah!

The host family are as we thought. There is one boy called William who is eleven years old. They have one mother at least and also one father. And then there is The Baby. It has a name, Sam, but it is usually referred to as The Baby. It is a monstrous thing, even uglier than the fully grown ones, but more on that later. It hasn't been with the family that long but already it has taken over the house and is VERY annoying.

Your faithful warrior

Bumpfizzle

I can't say the host family gave me a great welcome when I arrived.

'Daniel!' the Mother said, looking at me. 'Your turn to bring in the washing. Hurry along!'

Bring in the *washing*? If she knew that she was talking to a VICIOUS ALIEN WARRIOR I think she might at least have said 'please'!

I did bring in the stupid washing.

I only hope that my people on Plonk never find out. It does not look good for a famous warrior to be seen carrying under-garments and suchlike.

Annoying Baby Trait 1

The Baby talks utter rubbish but everyone has to listen to him.

Baby: Coo … dribble … blah!

Mother: Did you hear that? He's trying to talk!

The hoover has a better line in conversation.

OCTOBER 17TH

I have discovered that there is another small brother called Sooty. Sooty is very different to the other family members. He has four legs, is covered in fur and has a tail. (Actually he looks a lot like the Great Master's assistant Mrs Waggle on one of her good days.) He is not a very likable person. He spits. He also scratches. I have no idea why the Mother likes him so much. What is he but a furry bag full of guts?

(The Baby also spits and scratches and the Mother seems to like him too.)

I nearly forgot: humans go to the toilet INDOORS! Isn't that hilarious? The Father got very agitated this morning when I peed in the garden. As if there was only one way of doing things in the ENTIRE UNIVERSE. Humans!

OCTOBER 18TH

There are some DANGEROUS things on Earth. I told the Great Master all about them in my report this morning. This is what I wrote:

To: Planet Plonk
From: Warrior Bumpfizzle the Best

Oh Great Master of the Small Foot[1]

You were so wise, oh great one, to send a scout such as myself to check out this planet. Already, I have observed a potentially dangerous beast.

←----FLASHPOINT!----→
←----DANGER! DANGER!----→

---

1 He likes to be called that even though the truth is his feet are like spades.

(This is how I will alert you to danger, oh Great Master!)[2]

As I descended from the capsule, I was confronted by a large brute wearing a black and white skin. This animal is truly horrifying, oh brave master! It opened its mouth, on seeing this warrior, and roared. A terrifying sound! I knew at once that it was a kill-or-be-killed situation. I took a defensive position and launched a mighty kick.

Pow! Katunk!

The beast didn't move. It looked at me with hatred in its eyes T turned and made a daring escape over a stone wall and on to the road. I have since discovered a name for this savage.

He is known as A COW. The brother person William insists

2   Sometimes you have to really spell things out for him despite his great brain.

that cows are not dangerous and that I am a wuss for thinking that they were, which only proves, oh majestic one, how little the brother person knows.

*** ADVICE! ***

Warriors should carry a stun-gun to deal with such encounters.

I will continue to observe and
report back tomorrow.

You can depend on

Your faithful servant

Bumpfizzle the Best

OCTOBER 19TH

I have taken careful note of what humans eat. I like many things but so far the tastiest is the stuff in Sooty's bowl. (William dared me to eat it and being a warrior I cannot turn down such a challenge.) I especially like the pork and liver flavour.

In the future I imagine that the humans will probably want to honour me. I think a statue would be nice. I must remember to ask them to concentrate on my right side and to leave out my uneven snort-hole. They will call me *Bumpfizzle the Best, The Humans' Hero!*

I can't wait to see the look on Whizzpiffle's face.

She has been jealous of me since we were both in the nursery. That is why she and her gang don't like me. Wait till she sees the statue. She will be furious. She is the Great Master's niece but being well connected doesn't get you EVERYTHING you want. But enough about her, let's get back to me.

I have taken the liberty of writing a little song in praise of … well … of me!

Hail Bumpfizzle the mighty warrior!
Hail Bumpfizzle so fair of face
Hail Bumpfizzle the humans' hero
Mighty Bumpfizzle from another race
Hail Bumpfizzle from Planet Plonk
Hail Bumpfizzle so small of nose
Hail Bumpfizzle the perfect Plonker
Hail Bumpfizzle of the three short toes

OCTOBER 20TH

This morning, after breakfast (cereal and eggs for some, jellied eel for Sooty, both tasty), Will suggested that we play a game called 'Hide and Seek'. He had some friends over and they were eager to play. It is not a complicated game. One earthling hides and the others search for him. It is very like the wonderful Plonk game 'Find Your Head'.

William was first to be hunter. He went to his room to give us twenty seconds to hide. That is when I had a surge in head-noggin power. I rushed up the stairs and turned the key in his door thus protecting the family from him. The others hid. I did not see the need to, as I knew the hunter was going nowhere. After thirty mano tick tocks or so, the others reappeared. Instead of being grateful, they were furious. They released William and he threw himself on

14

me. Luckily, I am a highly trained warrior. I fought him off bravely and then sent for the Mother to suppress him. I was lucky to escape with my life.

'You're a cheat!' William said.

Me? A cheat? Whatever can that mean?

Annoying Baby Trait 2

Baby lies on blanket, smiling. Mother rushes to get camera. Mother points camera at baby. Baby cries. It does it ON PURPOSE.

OCTOBER 21ST

I have not the strength to write in my diary. I only just managed to write my report home.

To: Planet Plonk
From: Warrior Bumpfizzle the Best

Great Master of Many Head-Noggins!

Greetings from Earth.

Today I have discovered something very important. The 'Sooty' I talked about in my last report is not in fact human at all! This enormous furry creature with sharp claws and very bad breath called Sooty is what the family refer to as a 'pet'. He is no pet as we know pets, but a vicious predator – a cat.

Only this morning, I heard Mom (the Mother) say that he

is to be kept away from me, at all costs. 'I'm afraid Sooty has taken a dislike to Daniel,' the Mother said to the Father.

How clever the Mother is! That cat knows that I am not human. The Father was his usual sarcastic self.

'He's afraid of the cat now? I thought it was just cows. I give up!'

Can you send me some research about cats, oh Master of the Great Brain?

←----FLASHPOINT!----→

←----DANGER! DANGER!----→

Our memory-adjustor does not work on animals.

ADVICE

Use stun gun. See Cow.

Finally, oh Great One, I will no longer eat Sooty's food. As you know, I have a delicate stomach and his food does not agree with me. Excuse me, I think I am going to throw up again.

Your warrior

Bumpfizzle the Best

OCTOBER 22ND

Feeling a little better today. I only threw up twice. The Mother wanted to know what I had eaten so I told her.

'You ate the cat's food?' she said and her own face turned a little green. I didn't know I could pass this illness on.

Now I am not allowed to touch the cat's food and the Mother thinks that I am a total noodle. The cat looked at me in a very evil way.

I will need to be very careful around Mr Sooty.

OCTOBER 23RD

I am in constant danger in this house. The cat follows me around watching my every move. William kicks me whenever I refuse to go along with his plans. The Baby thinks the whole world revolves around him and takes up all the parents' time.

Only the Mother is truly kind to me. I had to train her, of course. I have developed a way of communicating with her. When I need her, I wobble my bottom lip and then look at the floor whilst wringing my hands together. This works very well. She comes and feeds me or saves me from the other children.

The Father is a different story. Sometimes, the Mother has to go out and she leaves the Father in charge of us. Every time he sees me he says: 'Shouldn't you be outside in the fresh air?' He doesn't understand that I am an INDOORS person. A curl-up-on-the-sofa person, a play-Scrabble person, a talk-to-the-Mother person.

As a warrior my life is full of stress. I need to be able to relax.

I try to communicate with him in my normal manner, lip wobbling, eyes on floor, hand wringing, but it does not work. He just ignores me as though I were a Dung-fabble beetle or an annoying Hobblebob-ble. What to do? What to diddly diddly do? I will continue to observe.

OCTOBER 24TH

To: Bumpfizzle
From: Whizzpiffle on Planet Plonk

RESEARCH ON CAT

CAT: Large wild animal from Africa or Asia. Predator. Man-eating. (Only a total nit-wit wouldn't know that.)

I wrote to the Master thanking him for the research into the cat. I had to say it was wonderful information, because if I'd said that Whizzpiffle is about as clever as a sofa, he would have got annoyed. No point in annoying him. I did not sleep for a long time last night. I kept thinking about the cat. A large wild animal. A man-eater. It is clear to me now that the Mother here has no idea what she is dealing with. She picks the cat up and holds it on her lap, rubs its head and

23

mollycoddles it. She feeds it saucers of milk and gives it food.

I knew I had to act! I got rid of the fierce cat. With no thought for my own safety, I put it in a bag and carried it to the park where I placed it in the bin. The Mother and host family are safe once more.

Annoying Baby Trait 3

When another child in the family does a FANTASTIC painting of another planet, The Baby pees in its nappy so that the Father has to change it, and cannot discuss the painting PROPERLY with the other child.

OCTOBER 26™

There was much excitement here today when the family hosted what they call a 'birthday'. It was The Baby's birthday and he was celebrating the number one. He is now one Earth winter old. This must be a very important number because they put it everywhere, even on their food. Not happy with that, they then made a ceremonial fire on top of the cake and sang to the number. Very strange. What is so cool about it? It's only one.

Then, they played music and fought over chairs. I do not understand this. There were many chairs in the house. One for each person, but not all chairs are equal and they all fought over these five special chairs. William cheated of course, pushing me out of the way so that I could not grab a chair. I complained to the Father but he ignored me and told the Mother that I was becoming a total nuisance.

But the most peculiar thing of all is the strange couple who have arrived at the house. The children call them 'Granny' and 'Granddad'.

Let me deal with Granny first. She is quite small but very round and she smells like the inside of a wardrobe. Every time she comes near The Baby she makes strange faces and says: 'Coocheecoocheecooo.'

Then she sprays his head with spit. I think she is speaking in some other language so I have no idea what she wants from him. I will continue to try to engage her in conversation and in that way find out more.

The Granddad looks like a normal human but with some strange features.

1. There are two enormous bushes growing over his peepholes.

2. He is constantly talking about fish. He is a fish hunter apparently.

3. He drinks a strong-smelling liquid every evening which makes him sing. (The singing resembles that of the Lesser Spotted Dingle Fish on our own beloved planet.)

4. He thinks that he is a very good cook. He decided to cook dinner for everyone while he was here. He said that I was his

volunteer helper. (This is strange because I did not volunteer.) He sent me to the shed to bring in onions. The dinner was quite tasty. Even the onions. Then the Father went berserk. Apparently, the onions I found in the shed were not onions but DAFFODIL BULBS. Who knew? William made things worse by saying that in spring we'll all have sunny daffodils shooting out of our behinds. The parents were not amused. After spending three hours at the emergency room in the hospital they were in no mood for jokes. We do not have onions or daffodils on Plonk. Therefore, it was not my fault. I am an alien.

NOTE TO SELF

Beware of older humans. They are not as
innocent as they look.
Use stun gun. See Cow.

Also, birthday cake and jelly and chocolate buns are all quite tasty but if eaten together in large portions they will make you VOMIT. Trust me, I know.

OCTOBER 27TH

The Mother has reported the cat missing. She rang the police. Police on Earth hunt for missing cats, it seems. Police on Plonk hunt for criminals. Another difference between our two planets.

This morning, the mother handed me a big pile of posters.

'Daniel!' she said. 'Go and put up these posters. We have to find poor Sooty!'

'Why?' I said.

She looked at me like I was a crazy alien.

'Because we want him back, Daniel! Don't we?'

'He is a dangerous predator,' I said reasonably.

'Only of mice,' she said.

Really, the Mother is too innocent to live. She seems to have forgotten how he has torn my skin in the past, leaving me badly wounded. She has no idea that Sooty is a man-killer. But then, she has no idea that I am Bumpfizzle the Best either.

OCTOBER 28TH

I got a very huffy note from the Great Master today. He says that he is losing patience with me. He says that I am not sending back USEFUL information and that I must change my ways or be replaced. Replaced! Me? What to do? What to diddly diddly do? I cannot be replaced! Cannot go back to Plonk as a failure. Imagine how Whizzpiffle would enjoy that!

OCTOBER 29TH

Life is very complicated here. As well as having to worry about the Master, I have to put up with this family. The Mother is good but she is often occupied with The Baby, who seems intent on destroying her life. It keeps her awake at night in a most selfish way, demanding milk and doing unmentionable things in the nappy department. I worry about the Mother and try to find ways to make her life easier but no-one even notices! It is so strange to me that these people all live together. At home, we live in separate pods. One Plonker in each pod.

Here are some good things about that:

1. You can do whatever you like.

2. No-one bosses you.

3. You eat what you want.

4. Go to sleep when you want.

But here! There is always someone telling me what to do.

Of course I like some parts of my life here. I like bedtime. The Mother reads a story to The Baby and I listen in. It's usually about bears or caterpillars. Then she kisses me and says, 'Sleep tight!'

When she does that I get a very nice fuzzy feeling. We don't have that feeling on Plonk. I am not sure what it is. It may be a human illness, of course.

Then the Mother goes out and closes the door, and I turn myself off, and go to sleep – lying down!

OCTOBER 30TH

After listening to the Mother reading last night I started thinking about caterpillars and cats. And then I remembered a famous poem written by Professor Plump from Plonk. This is how it goes:

Is the caterpillar
The common caterpillar
In any way related to the cat?
If the cat were out to dinner
Would she know the caterpillar?
My friend and I will clarify the facts.
My caterpillar friend is no relation to
    the cat
She's never even met a tabby tom
And yet the name persists
One generation to the next
To which the caterpillar answers with
    aplomb,

'My name is Caterpillar! Caterpillar!
   Caterpillar!
Though I'm nothing whatsoever to the
   cat
I've been called a caterpillar (as a name
   it's quite a winner)
You can see it on my birth certificate.'
Therefore I conclude
With no intention of being rude
That the caterpillar could indeed be
   right
Her identity is safe
Known to all the Plonker race
And she's absolutely nothing to the
   cat!

Ah, Professor Plunk. What a genius!

OCTOBER 31ˢᵀ

I sent another report to the Grand Master. This one was full of information.

To: Planet Plonk
From: Warrior Bumpfizzle the Best

Oh Most Generous one!

Thank you for your latest message! I know I have made mistakes in the past and that not all of my missions have been successful. But enough about that, oh most patient one, let us get down to business as they say here on Earth.

←----BASIC FACTS----→

Humans breathe ox-again through their snort-holes, which are on the outside of their bodies. (I know! I laughed too!)

Humans eat other creatures. They eat vegetables. Yes! Even baby carrots. The green vegetables smell and taste like Wingzong poo but, if humans fail to eat them, they do not grow. (We could eat them, though, Master! Imagine us now but twenty times bigger. Slap my head and call me a feather duster but I think we would look very attractive. Could I be wrong?)

They have glass boxes in their homes that tell them what the other humans are doing. This is called TV and is more popular with older humans. Younger ones use primitive computers where they conduct wars with other beings or swop photos of their faces. The face area is called Instagram. I have my own Instagram account now. Check it out! I put up a great selfie yesterday and a photo of my breakfast.

(I LOVE porridge. I love it almost as much as Uncle Jassop loved earwigs. Remember his earwig soup? Like that - only better. Seriously!

←----FLASHPOINT!----→
←----DANGER! DANGER!----→

Warriors should use Instagram carefully, Master!

ADVICE

They should not befriend too many people. If they do, they will have to spend hours looking at other people's faces.

Hope my research has pleased you oh Great One.

Bumpfizzle

P.S. I just found out that this is a special day here on

Earth. When it got dark, they all dressed up as ghosts and ghouls and yes ... ALIENS! Then they fed one another sweets and other treats. What codswollop! Humans are very strange.

Annoying Baby Trait 4

When The Baby starts to crawl, you have to close the front door after you, EVEN if you are in a terrible hurry and have something VERY important to do. Otherwise, people yell at you.

NOVEMBER 1ST

I have a new friend. Her name is Lucy. Her mother is the Mother's friend. They came to the house yesterday and we hung out together. That's what Lucy calls it: hanging out. How interesting I must seem to her, and humorous. I am naturally funny. She is also quite pleasant for a human.

NOVEMBER 2ND

Oh woppy-dee-doo-dah! Disaster! This is the worst day of my life. The worst day of ANY of my lives. I woke up this morning and got this message from Plonk.

To: Bumpfizzle
From: Planet Plonk

AS YOU SEEM UNABLE TO DO YOUR JOB I MUST DO IT FOR YOU. ANSWER THE FOLLOWING QUESTIONS:

1. CAN WE EAT HUMANS?
2. HOW DO THEY TASTE?
3. ARE THEY DIFFICULT TO CATCH?

HUMANS ARE TO BE OUR NEW FOOD SOURCE.
WE NEED THIS INFORMATION.
THAT IS THE REAL REASON YOU WERE SENT TO EARTH.

GET ON WITH IT!

THE GREAT MASTER HORNSWOGGLE

Our new food source? Is he serious? My human family have no idea of the danger they are in. They have no idea that without ME their fates would be sealed. And yet, I see no sign of gratitude. None. Typical.

NOVEMBER 3ʀᴅ

This is not working out in the way I had hoped. I am totally flummoxed. I thought I was to explore Earth and send back information. I was to organise the meeting of human and Plonker. I knew that this would put me in terrible danger, but what did I care! I am a warrior! But that's not what it is about. I have been such a fool.

They want to EAT humans?
They expect ME to eat humans?

With my sensitive stomach? I should have known! The master has an enormous appetite. Some less loyal warriors say that he only thinks about food. (I could say the same about the human Father.) I do hope that is not true. I can't imagine why the Master would want to EAT humans. Wouldn't he like to get to know them? He

doesn't even know about Scrabble yet. What to do? What to diddly diddly do?

NOVEMBER 4TH

William showed me a horror film last night called: *Cool Cannibals Rise Again*. It did not frighten me. I am a warrior. Besides, my troubles are far more important. I keep looking

at the family here and imagining the Great Master eating them. I even dreamt about it last night. I must have screamed because the Father came running in.

'It's all right, Dan,' he said. 'Nothing to be afraid of. Just a bad dream. Too much imagination. That's your trouble.'

I did not like that remark about *too much* imagination, and I said so.

'Well, you've been playing aliens for weeks now,' the Father said.

Playing aliens! There is no point in arguing with humans, though. Once they get an idea like that into their head-noggins, nothing will shift it. So I maintained a dignified silence.

Then he brought me hot milk and we chatted about football till I fell asleep. (It didn't take long. I have no interest in football.)

NOVEMBER 5TH

The Mother has said that William and I are not allowed to watch horror movies late at night. Now William is tetchy with me. I cannot waste time on him. I have bigger hamsters to fry. This morning I sent the following report to my home planet. In it, I decided to distract the master. I told him all about Lucy, my new friend. In this way, I hope the master will forget his terrible plan.

To: Planet Plonk
From: Warrior Bumpfizzle the Best

Oh Most Kind and Handsome Master!

It grieves me to see that you are not happy with my progress. I have been working non-stop since my arrival and had hoped my work was valuable. I will deal with your questions at once.

Humans are not difficult to catch. I thought at first that the males are better at running, but I am wrong in that. I met a female this week who lives three houses from us. Her name is Lucy, though we all call her Lucky Luce because she loves to do competitions and win prizes. She has AMAZING blue eyes, oh Clever One. She loves to run and is faster than all the boys, even William who is also fast. She doesn't like boys,

she says, but I think she quite likes me. She giggles when I speak to her. (Giggling is a sort of high squeaky laugh, very like the call of the Lesser-Spotted Zebraffe bird, but not as dangerous.)

I hope that answers all your questions, oh High and Mighty One.

Your servant

Bumpfizzle

I am very hopeful that he will forget about the eating-humans plan. I am quite a picky eater at the best of times and could not eat something as ugly as a human.

NOVEMBER 6ᵀᴴ

Another terrible day! Woke up to a message from Plonk. The Master was in a terrible tantrum. He sounded like a wounded Hotfissle Bird. He has not forgotten his wish to eat humans. I wrote back at once.

To: Planet Plonk
From: Warrior Bumpfizzle the Best

Oh Golden One of the Three Short Toes!

Yes. You did ask me if humans are good to eat. And yes, I didn't answer you. Curse me for a useless servant! I do not know if they are good to eat as I haven't eaten one yet. I will of course, Majesty, eat one, in time. I think they would taste REALLY bad except maybe The Baby. The Baby could be tasty, very tasty indeed - if it were

```
clean, which it isn't, most of
the time.

Your dearest subject

Bumpfizzle
```

What am I to do now? The Master does not forget easily. He will not rest until he finds a way to eat humans. I could try the Mother, perhaps. Try to eat her, I mean. She smells lovely. She smells of cow pansies and plonc blossoms. But I don't want to hurt her.

I mean I don't want her screaming and drawing attention to me.

NOTE TO SELF

I am a warrior. I am not afraid of hurting people.

NOVEMBER 12TH

It has been a very hectic week. There was no time to write in my diary. To the amazement of my head-noggin, the children here go to a 'school' to be educated. The school has been closed for many weeks because of a dripping roof. It reopened last Thursday and, to my shock, I was expected to go there five days a week.

At first I tried to persuade the Father to let me stay at home but he insisted it was for my own good. I explained to him that through the fruit of the Haganboganberry, I had learnt all available information on one side of the solar system. Surely that was enough for life on Earth? The Mother laughed and called me 'a chip off the old block' – whatever that is.

School is the most ridiculous place. The teacher is a human! How funny is that?

I remembered my Master's instructions, however. I tasted a human.

I BIT THE TEACHER ON THE FIRST MORNING.

What a fuss that caused! They think the teacher is a very important person on planet Earth. Everyone said I shouldn't have bitten her. But I couldn't eat someone that I knew, now, could I? Anyway, I hadn't planned it. I was trying to bite an apple using no hands. The apple was on my desk. The teacher foolishly made a move to grab it and I chomped down on her arm instead of the fruit.

The teacher was very angry. Things have been a tad tense in school since. Especially since the teacher believes that there is no life outside of Earth. I tried to argue with her, but she just became more purple in the face. The parents were also angry. The Mother said she was disappointed. The Father said something about having my head examined.

And how did it taste? The flesh tasted sour and moldy with a slight aftertaste of Wingzang vomit. The blood tasted like blood. I now know that we would not like human flesh. In fact it is the worst food I have ever tasted.

NOTE TO SELF

Do not bite teachers.
Use stun gun. See Cow.

I will write to the Master and explain to him that humans are off the menu.

NOVEMBER 13ᵀᴴ
(FRIDAY THE 13ᵀᴴ)

This arrived today:

To: Bumpfizzle
From: Planet Plonk

BUMPFIZZLE!

MANY RELIABLE EXPERTS HAVE TOLD ME THAT HUMANS TASTE VERY NICE INDEED. I SEE NOW THAT YOUR HEAD-NOGGIN IS TOTALLY EMPTY AND FOR THAT REASON, I HAVE SENT OPERATIVE WHIZZPIFFLE TO TAKE OVER FROM YOU. SHE WILL TAKE THE FORM OF A MOUSE IN ORDER TO BE DISCREET. AS SOON AS SHE MAKES CONTACT YOU ARE TO RETURN HOME.

THE GRAND MASTER HORNSWOGGLE

NOVEMBER 14ᵀᴴ

To: Planet Plonk
From: Warrior Bumpfizzle the Best

Oh Lofty One of the Soft Voice!

What a pity you did not contact me sooner! If I had only known that Whizzpiffle was coming to Earth disguised as a mouse, I would have rescued her without any thought for my own safety.

Let me start at the beginning. It was Friday – Friday the 13th. The luckiest day in the year on Plonk. Not so much here. Anyway, I had just come from school when I heard the Father screaming in the kitchen. I ran in to see what terrible danger had befallen him.

'Mouse!' he screamed as soon as he saw me. 'Get your mother!'

I went to fetch the Mother person. She went quite pale when

she heard about the mouse and suggested I get the cat. (I had no idea that humans are terrified of so small an animal. But then being a very brave warrior myself I do not understand fear.)

When I got back to the kitchen, the Father was quite calm, drinking tea. Mr Sooty was on his lap licking his lips and looking quite satisfied. I am so sorry oh Many-Headed and Hatted One. I fear that the lovely Whizzpiffle is no longer with us. May she rest in peace. My heart is filled with sadness.

Your servant

Bumpfizzle the Best

NOVEMBER 21ST

What a week this has been! Whizzpiffle arrived three days ago disguised as a mouse. She is as troublesome as ever. Sadly, the cat did not eat her. (I am afraid the account I gave to the Great Master was slightly fictitious in this regard.) I managed to capture her and put her in the cage which used to hold the hamster person. This was necessary because she was intent on getting rid of me in a very hurtful way. Now, the cage is in my

room and Whizzpiffle is driving me out of my head-noggin. She wants to kill me of course, but what's new?

I will write to my Master again with a new eating solution. I will also suggest that there is no need to invade as I can deliver the food. I have no wish to have the Master breathing down my neck and bossing me around. I must write my next report very carefully.

NOVEMBER 22ND

To: Planet Plonk
From: Warrior Bumpfizzle the Best

Dear Splendiferous One!

I understand that you cannot think about food right now when your heart is full of sorrow for your dear niece, Whizzpiffle. No! She did not suffer. The cat ate her in one gulp. Dang him for a furry fiend!

I have been thinking about food for you, oh Great Master. If we cannot eat humans – and I don't think we can, they taste vile, and the Master has a very sophisticated taste bud – perhaps we could live on peanut butter and maple syrup poured over bananas? This is my favourite snack and I think the people of our planet would enjoy it very much.

There is no need for Your Greatness to come all the way here. I will send you a sample of the food tomorrow. You should be able to use your snort-hole extension to suck it up.

Can you remind me where the extra-terrestrial passages are situated? I seem to have lost that information.

Bowing to your higher intelligence

I remain

Bumpfizzle

NOVEMBER 23ʳᵈ

Not a good day. Going about my official business, I ACCIDENTALLY knocked over a pyramid. It was a pyramid of egg cartons in a supermarket. Hornswoggle of the Big Feet had written a nasty and quite hurtful note that morning. In it he said that the extra-terrestrial passages between our world and Earth are to be found in pyramids. Pyramids?

I went to the supermarket with William to fetch milk for the Mother. That was when I had the altercation with the eggs. Most of the eggs fell on a cranky old woman.

She roared the place down and hit me with her walking frame and when I tried to explain to the policeman, he got all bossy and said that I had no business going near the pyramid. What did he know? I told him he should be off searching for cats. He didn't like that. He said some very hurtful things. If only I could have revealed my true identity! How he would have shivered!

Of course the parents wanted to know WHY I interfered with the pyramid. And of course I could not tell them the truth. Mum was disappointed again. Dad was not pleased at all, and now, I am grounded. No matter! I am a warrior. I expect to suffer.

Annoying Baby Trait 5

Babies leak from both ends.

NOVEMBER 24TH

This came today from you know who:

```
WE HAVE RECEIVED NO FOOD YOU
USELESS OPERATIVE OF THE LARGE
SNORT-HOLE. THIS IS YOUR LAST
WARNING. I WILL TAKE NO MORE
FAILURE.

GREAT MASTER HORNSWOGGLE
```

Meanwhile I am still grounded, as is William, because he was at the supermarket with me, and no-one would believe that he wasn't involved. He says I'm dead as soon as he gets his hands on me. I am forced to stay at home reading books. I have found some good ones about the ancient Romans and Greeks. Slap my head and call me a feather duster but it seems that those old Romans and Greeks liked sacrificing things, especially goats. Interesting.

Only the Mother is sympathetic and even she thinks I am looking for notice, being the middle child. I heard her explain it all to the Father.

He said he'd give me some notice I didn't want if I ever embarrassed him like that again. He is a most difficult human. I am tempted to fry his ears but this might draw more attention to me.

And to add to my terrible misfortunes, the Master has now demanded a sacrificial goat to be offered to the gods. He thinks that this will cause food to suddenly appear. Who does he think he is? Nero? And where would I find a goat? His instructions are quite specific:

```
PLACE  FLOWERS  ON  THE  GOAT'S
HEAD.  THEN  AT  MIDNIGHT  CRUSH
HIS BONES AND DRINK HIS BLOOD.
```

Really? Crush his bones? With what? I cannot even think about the blood-drinking. What to do? What to diddley diddley do?

NOVEMBER 25TH

The most hammer-hopping thing has happened. Lucy (my friend) has won two tickets to the Picket Pet Farm and she has invited me to join her. What wondrous fortune! William was there at a birthday party Tuesday seven weeks ago and he told me that they have a goat there.

A goat! Oh Handsome Head of Utter Cleverness, I said to myself when I heard it. I will go there and send the stinking goat to the Master.

NOVEMBER 26TH

As I said, I know nothing about goats. We do not have such creatures on my planet, though the people of Planet Gardyloo have similar

hair growing from their chin-wobbles. I have done much research and can now recognise a goat without any great trouble.

William is annoyed that Luce invited me and not him, but I explained to him that Luce is a person of great taste and would never like a boy with sticking-out ears like his. William tried to push me down the stairs at that point, but the Mother saved me.

Luce texted me this morning to say that her big brother Trevor is coming with her. She is such a joker! She calls him her FEROCIOUS BODYGUARD. William laughed too when I told him. In fact, he couldn't stop laughing.

We leave in the morning.

NOVEMBER 27TH

What a terrible week! I will start at the beginning. I went to the pet farm with Luce and Trevor who is her brother. Trevor is as tall as a small tree

and as wide as a huggletoe mugaphant. He has hair on his noggin, in his lug-holes and up his snort-hole. There is also hair growing on the back of his hands. The hands are more like shovels, actually. They look like hands that were especially designed to hurt people.

It started off well. Luce was delighted to see me, and Trevor sat in front of us on the bus, and didn't talk. He was smelling though. Every three seconds, he emitted a blast of noxious gas from his backside. I pointed that out, politely of course, and from then on, he didn't seem to warm to me. Luce said he didn't like people talking about his backside. Who knew?

The real trouble began at the Picket Pet Farm. I will confess that I had no interest in the farm until we came to the goat. I let the others walk on ahead of me and I went to examine this curious animal.

There are pointy things growing on the head-noggin to hold the flowers so that is something, I suppose. There are some nice flowers in the park down the road from the house. I'm thinking roses and some green stuff. (See attached diagram.) I had no idea what the pointy things actually did, at the time. My plan was to befriend the goat and then lure him to his death as soon as I found

GOAT DIAGRAM

a full moon. I had an apple in my rucksack. I jumped over the fence and approached the goat. His name was Psycho. At that time, that meant nothing to me. It was not a word I knew. The goat looked at me. I looked at the goat.

I addressed him in my normal polite fashion, explaining to him that he was to be sacrificed for Planet Plonk. (On reflection, he probably didn't need to know that.) The goat went back to eating grass and ignored me. I offered him the apple. He continued eating. I MAY have poked him with a stick, at this point, to get his attention.

The goat turned around. His eyes were red. He lowered his head. The last thing I saw were the two pointy sharp things. Then I was flying through the air. I now knew what the two pointy sharp things were *for*.

I landed on top of Luce, who had come back to search for me. She was carrying a large ice-cream cone. A soon as I hit her she started to scream and spouted gallons of water from her peep-holes. The ice-cream exploded and covered most of my head-noggin. I tried to explain to Luce about the goat, but she wouldn't listen.

'What were you doing with that goat?' she asked. 'You're not playing "aliens" again, are you?'

Then Trevor came running up. He saw the blood flowing from Luce's knees and raised his great paw. Slap my face and call me a wiggly worm but didn't he hit me, when I wasn't looking, and knock me out. What a lucky boy he was! If I hadn't been uncon scious, I could have pulled his arms off and tied them around his neck like a scarf. Ha!

NOVEMBER 28TH

Today, the Master sent me a letter which included a terrible disease: the Flackin Pox. On Planet Plonk, it is easy-peasy to buy a disease, and put it in a letter. I am covered in spots and scabs and cannot stop itching. Can life get any worse?

The Mother is convinced I have chicken pox. William has chicken pox. Ruby next door has chicken pox. Even Lucky Luce has the pox.

Chicken pox is a holiday on a yacht, in the Mediterranean Sea, with servants and your own personal ice-cream machine, in comparison to Flackin Pox. I let her put cream on the scabs, though I licked it off afterwards. I tastes a bit like the Purple Hogganberry, but sweeter.

NOVEMBER 29TH

The cat has arrived back. Not dead as I hoped but alive and well and as mad as a Red Spitzinbaum with a sore throat. He is now outwardly aggressive towards me and follows me around giving me the evil eye.

William is out to cripple me at every opportunity. Only last evening, he kicked me under the table and I now have a massive bruise on top of one of my worst scabs. With all that going on, I haven't been able to get back to the farm to finish off the goat.

NOVEMBER 30TH

Whizzpiffle and the cat are now best friends. The cat spends his time lying on my bed chatting to her. They are constantly plotting against me. They get me into trouble at every turn but, so far, I have avoided major consequences. My nerves are frayed, though, and I am buckling under the stress.

Last night, The Baby was crying constantly and trying to grab the book I was reading. I took him out to the garden and left him there to play. Yes it was dark and it was raining, but rain won't melt him, will it? And I know there is a busy road outside but the gate was closed, as I explained to the Mother. The stupid Baby can hardly walk. Did she think he was going to climb over the gate like a cat? Such a fuss! The Mother said some very CRUEL things. It seems that she is VERY fond of that baby.

I don't care.

I am an alien.

The sooner I can exit this planet the better. I still don't know what His Lordship of the Thick Lips will have to say about the goat. He may force me to return to my own lovely pod and get away from the numb-noggins on Earth. I do hope so. Then the Mother will be sorry.

DECEMBER 1ST

To: Planet Plonk
From: Warrior Bumpfizzle the Best

Oh Most Handsome and Endearing Master!

I do apologise for not having found a goat to sacrifice. I will now answer all your other questions.

Firstly, The Baby. It has become very unpredictable. Only yesterday I tried to take back a biscuit which was rightfully mine and it bit me! I do not know if it planned to eat me but I took no chances. I hid under the high chair until the Mother came to rescue me.

Secondly, it weighs about 10kg. The fattest part of it are the legs.

I do hope my answers will please you oh most important one.

Your Bumpfizzle

Annoying Baby Trait 6

Has no idea what belongs to it and what DOES NOT!

DECEMBER 2ᴺᴰ

Shocking letter from the Master:

```
BUMPFIZZLE!

YOU ARE A WASTE OF SPACE. YOU
HAVE FAILED UTTERLY WITH THE
GOAT.
   I HAVE HAD TO MAKE ANOTHER
PLAN. YOU MUST SACRIFICE THE
BABY. AFTER THE SACRIFICE HAS
BEEN MADE, WE CAN EAT IT. FROM
WHAT YOU SAY IT IS NOW BIG ENOUGH
TO FEED AT LEAST ONE FAMILY.
   DO NOT FAIL! YOU DO NOT WISH
TO SEE MY WRATH!

GREAT MASTER H.
```

It looks like The Baby's days are numbered. What a pity! It will not be my fault. I, as a warrior, must follow orders. The parents will be distraught. But then, they will recover. Things will go back to the way they used to be before The Baby. The parents may even find reasons to thank me. They will have more time to hang out with their other children, for example.

Well, William, really.

I could not care less.

I am an alien.

DECEMBER 3ᴿᴰ

I had another narrow escape today! On my way to school I saw Trevor standing at the corner with a lighted stick in his mouth. I jumped behind a dustbin with an athletic leap. Luckily, he did not see me. I had to remain there for over two hours until I was sure the coast was clear. A warrior such as myself cannot take unnecessary risks. I arrived in school late and the teacher was wearing her most contrary face.

Before I could say anything, William told her that I had spent the morning at the dentist, which was a lie, but most welcome. I was very grateful to him but when I tried to hug and kiss him (a custom on Planet Earth) he kicked me. Still, I feel we are making progress.

Later, he invited me to play football with him and his friends. He said blood was thicker than water. (Who knew?) I only had to stand in goal and prevent the ball going past me. It was not an unpleasant experience although my head-noggin did get wet and it was difficult to concentrate on my book.

DECEMBER 4TH

No word from the Master. He seems to have forgotten about me for the moment. I am happy about that as things have improved here. The weather has turned bitterly cold and yesterday white, fluffy bits of sky rained down. People collected it and made statues of men or moulded it into balls and threw it at one another. I thought this very strange at first, but in the evening, when Dad came home, we all went outside and made statues and threw snowballs. The Baby had to stay inside. No-one was sorry. (Maybe they won't miss him as much as I first thought after the sacrifice.)

What larks we had! So much giggling and laughing out loud. Dad managed to put snow down the back of my jumper and Mum showed me how to make a snow angel. I even made a statue that looked like the Great Master with extra large lips. Earth is very different to Planet Plonk. In a good way.

DECEMBER 5TH

I have thought a lot about sacrificing The Baby. There are advantages and disadvantages. Our teacher says that it is always good to list the advantages and the disadvantages so that you see every side of the problem.

ADVANTAGES:

1. No annoying crying when watching favourite television programme

2. No having to listen to Mother person going on and on and on about how cute The Baby is

3. No having to be quiet while The Baby sleeps

4. More time for all the family to spend with parents

5. More time for parents to listen to their other children

DISADVANTAGES:

1. ...

DECEMBER 6TH

To: Planet Plonk
From: Warrior Bumpfizzle the Best

Dear Master of the Honeyed Breath

I am working on a plan to kidnap
The Baby and sacrifice him, Your
Greatness. Please be patient.

Your servant

Bumpfizzle

DECEMBER 7TH

I am confused by The Baby. It seems to like me now. It squeezes my finger when I go near it which is a surprisingly pleasant sensation and it doesn't scream as much as it used to. (Has it heard about the sacrifice?)

DECEMBER 10TH

To: Bumpfizzle
From: Planet Plonk

YOU MANGY BLOCKHEADED STINKING DIM-WIT! WHERE IS THE BABY? THREE DAYS WE HAVE WAITED! I HAVE BEEN FORCED TO EAT BEETLES AND HOGGLEPOT STEW! THIS IS YOUR LAST CHANCE. MAKE THAT SACRIFICE! APPEASE THE GODS! WE ARE GETTING HUNGRIER BY THE HOUR.

THE GREAT MASTER HORNSWOGGLE

What to do? What to diddly diddly do? This is a disaster! Two days ago The Baby got out of the cage they keep him in, and managed to push the cat, Mr Sooty, into the microwave. Slap my face and call me a wiggly worm, but didn't the microwave explode! The cat almost was no more, but escaped with a shorter tail, no eyelashes and a strong smell of smoke coming from him, every time he moves.

The Baby's plan may have failed but it was a MOST CUNNING plan. Even I never thought of doing such a thing. I see now that The Baby has some useful purposes.

I still hate that cat.

DECEMBER 11TH

The Baby fell asleep on me today. I was lying on the sofa reading my book and it climbed on top of me. Within seconds it had switched itself off. It was a most pleasant sensation. When it is asleep The Baby is warm and heavy and makes tiny little breathing noises.

Then my hand went to sleep. (The Baby was lying on it.)

This was not quite as pleasant. None the less, I don't think ANYONE should EVER eat a baby.

I will write to the Master and explain this. I will tell him that The Baby can be annoying but has some good qualities. I will describe how cuddly it is and how little bubbles come out of its mouth when it laughs. It is easy to make it laugh. It especially laughs if you blow raspberries on its face or its tummy.

It is not available for sacrifices.

I will write the letter now.

Annoying Baby Trait 7

Babies have no talents, no skills and no brain but they are fun in their own way. This makes no sense and confuses other people.

DECEMBER 12TH

To: Planet Plonk
From: Warrior Bumpfizzle the Best

Oh Great Master of the Hairy Left Leg

Please calm down! There is no need to invade. NO NEED! Please be patient, oh Hungry One of the Tiny Mouth!

Your hard-working servant

Bumpfizzle

I thought that would work. I thought it would calm him down. Then this arrived.

To: Bumpfizzle
From: Planet Plonk

PREPARE EARTH FOR INVASION. SUGGEST SHAPE FOR US TO TAKE. ANSWER QUICKLY OR PREPARE TO BE

ANNIHILATED! THIS IS YOUR LAST
WARNING!

THE GREAT MASTER HORNSWOGGLE

What a to-do! When I got that last message
I went straight to Whizzpiffle. What choice
did I have? She knows him better than
anyone. She says the Master will invade.
He is probably preparing an army RIGHT
NOW! She also said that he will tear me
apart, crush my bones and make black
pudding from my blood, if I don't answer
him!

He will also destroy The Baby.

(She and the cat are new best friends and
want to run away together possibly to Planet
Cattywampus, for obvious reasons. She
knows that if her cousin the Great Master
Hornswoggle comes to Earth, he will put
an end to her plans.)

We spent all night trying to come up with a solution but all our answers needed help from a human. What to diddly diddly do?

DECEMBER 13TH

To: Bumpfizzle
From: Planet Plonk

PREPARE EARTH FOR INVASION. WILL
TAKE SHAPE OF POISONOUS SNAKES.
PREPARE TO BE ANNIHILATED! THIS
IS YOUR LAST WARNING!

THE GREAT MASTER HORNSWOGGLE

DECEMBER 14TH

Today is a MOMENTOUS day. After the last message from Hornswoggle I told William and Lucy who I REALLY was! I know. Exciting! They were shocked, of course. Luce laughed, which is how humans react to shock. William said that he already knew because he had been reading my diary. (Note to self: Punish William for reading very private diary.)

Between us we have come up with a plan. I am crossing all my fingers, toes and inner tentacles that it will work.

'First,' Lucy said, 'they can't come as snakes. They could easily wipe out the humans with their venom!'

'What about kittens?' William said. 'Everyone loves kittens and they couldn't do any harm to the humans.'

Sometimes, William is VERY smart.

DECEMBER 15TH

To: Planet Plonk
From: Warrior Bumpfizzle the Best

Dear Master

I look forward to your invasion.

←----FLASHPOINT!----→
←----DANGER! DANGER!----→

Do NOT come in form of snake. Humans do not fear snakes. They dance on their heads, they crush them under their heels. Please come in the form of a kitten. A kitten is a very ferocious and dangerous animal. They are even more wild and ferocious than fully grown cats. Humans are terrified of them. They are also the ugliest creatures on the planet. Because they are so ferocious, the humans bring them gifts of food at all times, but especially this time of year. Kittens can rip humans apart in five nano tick tocks. Do not fear, oh great and very brave one, I will prepare a great welcome for you and your army. Some useful phrases for you:

Meow meow: Give me food!

Meow meow meow meow: Die, human!

Meow!: I am now your King and Master!

Salutsan!

Bumpfizzle

DECEMBER 16TH

What a risky plan! This may be my last chance to write in this diary. I am so nervous I have developed a tic in my face. I twitch every time I think of the Master. Mum thinks I need a tonic. I know nothing about tonics. I only know one thing. I would die to protect this family – even The Baby.

We are on phase two of the great plan. William has gone on Facebook with this notice:

FREE
Live kittens! Extra cute.
Out of this World!
Just in time for Christmas!
Call to 34 Fordbroad
Crescent,Teerbally to collect.
Bring kitten food.
Available from 8am.
Perfect for Christmas

Annoying Baby Trait 8

I'm sure there is one. I just can't seem to remember what it is.

DECEMBER 18TH

It is over! At 8am today I was up and waiting in our front garden. The street was as quiet as the burp of a Hissboorah Lizard. William and Lucy had put signs all over town about the free kittens but it seemed that no-one had turned up.

Suddenly, I heard a loud noise. *Meow! Meow! Meow!*

The Great Master had arrived with an army of one hundred furry warriors all mewling

and yowling and hissing in their little kitten voices. The noise!

With that, the Mother and The Baby came to the door to see what all the fuss was about. My heart sank. The Master stepped forward. I recognised him at once. Even shaped as a kitten you could see that he had fat lips. The Master's beady little eyes lit up. He tottered over to the mother, his whiskers all a-quiver.

'Kitty!' The Baby called.

The Master raised a tiny clawed foot and hissed.

I threw myself on top of him and knocked him to the ground. My nose was full of fur. My eyes were running. The Master scratched me viciously with his claws. (Curse me for an empty head-noggin noodle, I should have told him to remove the claws before the invasion.)

He went for my throat. At that very second, an enormous crowd of people appeared at the top of the road. Many of them carried bowls full of kitten food.

The Master smelt the food. He stopped. He stood up. The crowd grew so excited when they saw the cute little kittens. They launched themselves at them.

The kitten-warriors called out the phrases I had taught them. The Master was one of the first to be trapped. The people were delighted that the kittens were so easy to catch. The warriors were delighted that there was so much food. There were baskets and collars and fur and kittens everywhere!

By 9am there wasn't a kitten to be seen.

The last I heard from the Master he was calling my name in a most unfriendly way. It sounded like he was trying to cough up a fur ball. He was also demanding more food. (Though no human understood a word he said of course!) His captor was an itsy-bitsy girl in a yellow dress. Last time I saw him, the girl was putting a pink collar on him and had named him Frufru.

DECEMBER 22ND

Things have returned to normal here now. It will be Christmas Eve in two more sleeps. I can't wait! Apparently on Christmas Eve another alien-type creature comes down the chimney here bearing gifts. I shall wait up that night and meet him. I am sure he will find me fascinating.

I will stay here on Earth now. Whizzpiffle and Sooty have departed for Cattywampus and I miss them a little but they have promised to come and visit often.

I am busy making presents for the family. So far, here is what I have:

1. Two knitted socks for the Father (pink with blue dots).

2. A bottle of Plonk perfume for the mother with garlic and some old fish. Lovely.

3. Sticky tape for William to help with the sticky-out ears.

4. And for The Baby? I am building a replica of the Mother for him to hang out of. It will leave the Mother free for her other-children important activities.

Lucy and I are best friends again. She helped us decorate our tree yesterday. She put the tree up inside the house! How funny Luce is! Trees do not live indoors. Dang her for a silly Cobblewoggle! I will move it to the garden tonight.

I had to do a memory wipe on her and on William so they are back to thinking I am a normal boy instead of Bumpfizzle the Best. This of course means that they have no idea that I single-handedly overcame the great Master Hornswoggle and his terrible army. Ah well, such is the fate of warriors.

DECEMBER 23ᴿᴰ

To: Planet Plonk
From: Warrior Bumpfizzle the Best

If there is anyone left up there could you possibly add me to the list of famous warriors of Plonk? I have dreamed for many years of being mentioned there. If you could use the image of me with my right snort-hole thrown over my shoulder perhaps?

No news from here. We were expecting the Great Master but he hasn't shown up yet. I await further instructions.

Salutsan!

Warrior Bumpfizzle the Humans' Hero

ABOUT THE AUTHOR

Patricia Forde is from Galway in the west of Ireland. She has published many books for children and has written plays and television drama. She has a husband and two teenage children. None of them are aliens to the best of her knowledge.

ABOUT THE ILLUSTRATOR

Elīna Brasliņa is an illustrator from Latvia. She has illustrated thirteen titles, most of them children's books and young adult novels. Elīna's work has been nominated for local awards and the Kate Greenaway Medal, and she has twice received the Zelta Ābele Award for Book Design, as well as the Jānis Baltvilks Baltic Sea Region Award in 2017.

ABOUT THE PUBLISHER

Based in Dublin, Little Island Books has been publishing books for children and teenagers since 2010. It is Ireland's only English-language publisher that publishes exclusively for young people. Little Island specialises in publishing new Irish writers and illustrators, and also has a commitment to publishing books in translation.

www.littleisland.ie